William and the School Report and Other Stories

Richmal Crompton, who wrote the original *Just William* stories, was born in Lancashire in 1890. The first story about William Brown appeared in *Home* magazine in 1919, and the first collection of William stories was published in book form three years later. In all, thirty-eight William books were published, the last one in 1970, after Richmal Crompton's death.

Martin Jarvis, who has adapted the stories in this book for younger readers, first discovered *Just William* when he was nine years old. He made his first adaptation of a William story for BBC radio in 1973 and since then his broadcast readings have become classics in their own right. BBC Worldwide have released nearly a hundred William stories on audio cassette and for these international best-sellers Martin has received a Gold Disc and the British Talkies Award. An award-winning actor, Martin has also appeared in numerous stage plays, television series and films.

All *Meet Just William* titles can be ordered at
your local bookshop or are available by post
from Book Service by Post (tel: 01624 675137).

Meet

Just William

William and the School Report and Other Stories

Adapted from Richmal Crompton's
original stories by Martin Jarvis

Illustrated by Tony Ross

MACMILLAN CHILDREN'S BOOKS

First published 2000 by Macmillan Children's Books
a division of Macmillan Publishers Limited
20 New Wharf Road, London N1 9RR
Basingstoke and Oxford
www.panmacmillan.com

Associated companies throughout the world

ISBN 0 330 39211 5

3 5 7 9 8 6 4

A CIP catalogue record for this book is available from
the British Library.

Typeset by SX Composing DTP, Rayleigh, Essex
Printed and bound in Great Britain by Mackays of Chatham plc, Kent

Contents

Dear Reader

Ullo. I'm William Brown. Spect you've heard of me an' my dog Jumble cause we're jolly famous on account of all the adventures wot me an' my friends the Outlaws have.

Me an' the Outlaws try an' avoid our famlies cause they don' unnerstan' us. Specially my big brother Robert an' my rotten sister Ethel. She's awful. An' my parents are really <u>hartless</u>. Y'know, my father stops my pocket-money for no reason at all, an' my mother never lets me keep pet rats or <u>anythin'</u>.

It's jolly hard bein' an Outlaw an' havin' adventures when no one unnerstan's you, I can tell you.

You can read all about me, if you like, in this excitin' an' speshul new collexion of all my fav'rite stories. I hope you have a jolly gud time readin' 'em.

Yours truly

William Brown

William and the School Report

It was the last day of term. School had broken up, and William was making his slow and gloomy way homeward. The prospect of holiday coaching loomed ominously ahead.

It would do William, said the headmaster enthusiastically, all the good in the world. Nothing like individual coaching. Nothing at all.

William's father was impressed. He saw a peaceful period during which William, daily occupied with his hour of coaching and its complement of homework, would lack both time and spirit to spread around him the devastation that usually marked the weeks of the holiday.

He thanked the headmaster profusely, and said that he would let him know definitely later on.

"In the *holidays*," William exclaimed on being confronted with the suggestion by his father. "There's lors against it. I'm sure there's lors against it. I've never heard of anyone having lessons in the holidays. Not anyone! I bet even *slaves* didn't have lessons in the holidays. I bet if they knew about it in Parliament there'd be an inquest about it. Besides, I shall only get ill with overworkin' an' get brain fever same as they do in books, an' then you'll have to pay doctors' bills, an' p'raps you'll have to pay for my funeral too. I don't see how anyone could go on workin' like that for months an' months without ever stoppin' once an' not get brain fever and die of it. Anyone'd think you wanted me to die. An' if I did die, I shun't be surprised if the judge did something to you about it."

His father, unmoved by this dark hint, replied, coolly, "I'm quite willing to risk it." But always a fair man, he continued, "I'll make no arrangements till I've seen your report. If it's a better one than it usually is, of course, you needn't have holiday coaching."

But in his pocket William now carried the worst report he had ever had. Disregarding (in common with the whole school) the headmaster's injunction to give the report to his parents without looking at it first, he had read it apprehensively in the cloakroom and it had justified his blackest fears.

He walked slowly and draggingly. His father would demand the report – and at once make arrangements for the coaching. The weeks of the holidays stretched – an arid desert – before him.

To make things worse, an aunt of his father's (whom William had not seen for several years) was coming over for the day, and William considered that his family was always more difficult to deal with when there were visitors.

Having reached the road in which his home was, he halted – irresolute. His father was coming home for lunch because of the aunt. He might be at home now.

The moment when the report should be demanded was, in William's opinion, a moment to be postponed as far as possible. He turned aside into a wood, and wandered on aimlessly.

"If ever I get into Parliament," he muttered fiercely, "I'll pass a lor against reports."

Suddenly, as he turned a bend in the path, he came face to face with an old lady. He was about to pass her hurriedly when she accosted him.

"I'm afraid I've lost my way, little boy," she said breathlessly. "I was directed to take a short cut from the station to the village, through the wood, and I think I must have made a mistake."

William looked at her. "What part of the village d'you want to get to?" he said curtly.

"Mr Brown's house," said the old lady. "I'm expected there for lunch."

The horrible truth struck William. This was his father's aunt, who was coming over for the day. He was about to give her hasty directions and turn to flee from her, when he saw that she was peering at him with an expression of delighted recognition.

"But it's William," she said. "I remember you quite well. I'm your Aunt Augusta. What a good thing I happened to meet you, dear! You can take me home with you."

William was disconcerted for a moment. They were, in reality, only a very short distance from his home. But it was no part of William's plan to return home at once.

He considered the matter for a minute, then said, "All right. You c'n come along with me."

"Thank you, my dear boy," said the old lady, "thank you. That will be very nice. I shall quite enjoy having a little talk with you. It's several years since I met you, but, of course, I recognised you at once."

William shot a suspicious glance at her, but it was evident that she intended no personal insult. She was smiling at him benignly.

Aunt Augusta discoursed brightly as William led her further and further into the heart of the wood and away from his home. She told him stories of her far-off childhood, describing in great detail her industry and obedience and love of study.

"There's no joy like the joy of duty done, dear boy," she said. "I'm sure you know that."

"Uh-huh," said William shortly.

As they proceeded on into the wood, however, she grew silent and rather breathless. "Are we – nearly there, dear boy?" she said.

They had almost reached the end of the wood, and another few minutes would have brought them out into the main road where a bus would take them to within a few yards of William's home. William still had no intention of going home. He felt sure that there was a solution if only he could think of it.

He sat down abruptly on a fallen tree, and said casually, "I'm afraid we're lost. We must've took the wrong turning. This wood goes on for miles an' miles. People've sometimes been lost for days."

"With – with no food?" said Aunt Augusta faintly.

"Yes, with no food."

Aunt August gave a little gasp.

But William's heart was less stony then he liked to think.

"Look here," he said, "I think p'raps that path'll get us out. Let's try that path."

"No," she panted. "I'm simply exhausted. I can't walk another step just now. Besides, it might only take us further into the heart of the wood."

"Well, I'll go," said William. "I'll go an' see if it leads to the road."

"No, you certainly musn't," said Aunt Augusta sharply. "We must at all costs keep together. You'll miss your way, and we shall both be lost separately. I've read of that

8

happening in books. I forbid you going a yard without me, William, and I'm too much exhausted to walk any more, just at present."

William who was by now tiring of the adventure hesitated, then said vaguely, "Well . . . s'pose I leave some sort of trail, same as they do in books."

"But what can you leave a trail of?" said Aunt Augusta.

Suddenly William's face shone as if illuminated by a light within. "I've got an envelope in my pocket," he said. "I'll tear that up. I mean . . ." he added cryptically, "it's a case of life and death, isn't it?"

"Do be careful then, dear boy," said Aunt Augusta anxiously. "Drop it every inch of the way. I hope it's something you can spare, by the way?"

"Oh yes," William assured her, "it's something I can spare all right."

He took the report out of the pocket and began to tear it into tiny fragments. He walked slowly down the path, dropping the pieces, and taking the precaution of tearing each piece into further fragments as he dropped it. There must be no possibility of its being rescued and put together again.

The path led, as William had known it would, round a corner and immediately into the main road. He returned a few minutes later, having assumed an expression of intense surprise and delight.

"'Sall right," he announced, "the road's jus'

round there."

Aunt Augusta took out a handkerchief and mopped her brow.

"I'm so glad, dear boy," she said. "So very glad. What a relief! I was just wondering how one told edible from inedible berries. We might, as you said, have been here for days . . . Now let's just sit here and rest a few minutes, before we go home. Is it far by the road?"

"No," said William. "There's a bus that goes all the way."

He took his seat by her on the log, trying to restrain the exuberant expansiveness of his grin. His fingers danced a dance of triumph in his empty pockets.

"I was so much relieved, dear boy," went on Aunt Augusta, "to see you coming back again. By the way, what was the paper that you tore up, dear? Nothing important, I hope?"

William had his face well under control by now. "It was my school report," he said. "I was jus' takin' it home, when I met you."

He spoke sorrowfully, as one who has lost his dearest treasure.

Aunt Augusta's face registered blank horror. "You – you tore up your school report?"

"I had to," said William. "I'd rather," he went on, assuming an expression of noble self-sacrifice, "I'd rather lose my school report, than have you starve to death."

"But – your school report, dear boy," she said. "It's dreadful to think of your sacrificing that for me. I remember so well the joy and pride of the moment when I handed my school report to my parents. I'm sure you know that moment well."

William, not knowing what else to do, heaved a deep sigh.

"Was it," said Aunt Augusta, still in a tone of deep concern and sympathy, "was it a specially good one?"

"We aren't allowed to look at them," said William unctuously. "They always tells us to take them straight home to our parents without looking at them."

"Of course. Of course, quite right, of course, but – oh, how disappointing for you, dear boy. You have some idea, no doubt, what sort of report it was?"

"Oh yes," said William, "I've got some sort of an idea all right."

"And I'm sure, dear," said Aunt Augusta, "that it was a very, very good one."

William's expression of complacent modesty was rather convincing. "Well . . . I – I dunno," he said self-consciously.

"And that tells me that it was," said Aunt August triumphantly. "I like a boy to be modest about his attainments. I don't like a boy to go about boasting of his successes in school. I'm sure you never do that, do you, dear boy?"

"Oh no," said William, with perfect truth. "No, I never do that."

"But I'm so worried about the loss of your report. How quietly and calmly you sacrificed it. Couldn't we try to pick up the bits on our way to the road and piece them together for

13

your dear father to see?"

"Yes," said William. "Yes, we could try 'n' do that."

He spoke brightly, happy in the consciousness that it couldn't possibly be put together.

They went slowly along the little path that led to the road.

Aunt Augusta picked up the "oo" of "poor" and said, "This must be a 'good', of course." She picked up the "ex" of "extremely lazy and inattentive" and said, "this must be an 'excellent', of course." But even Aunt Augusta realised that it would be impossible to put together all the pieces.

"I'm afraid it can't be done, dear," she said sadly. "How disappointing for you. I know just what you are feeling, dear boy."

William, hoping that she didn't, hastily composed his features to their expression of complacent modesty tinged with deep disappointment – the expression of a boy who has had the misfortune to lose a magnificent school report . . .

His father was at home, and came to the front door to greet Aunt Augusta. "Hello!" he said. "Oh – picked up William on the way?"

He spoke without enthusiasm. He wasn't a mercenary man, but this was his only rich unmarried aunt, and he'd hoped that she wouldn't see too much of William on her visit.

Aunt Augusta at once began to pour out a long and confused account of her adventure. "And we were completely lost . . . right in the heart of the wood. I was too much exhausted

to go a step farther, but this dear boy went on to explore and, solely on my account, because I was nervous of our being separated, he tore up his school report to mark the trail. It was, of course, a great sacrifice for the dear boy, because he was looking forward with such pride and pleasure to watching you read it."

William gazed into the distance as if he saw neither his father nor Aunt Augusta. Only so could he retain his expression of patient suffering.

"Oh, he was, was he?" said Mr Brown sardonically, but in the presence of his aunt forebore to say more.

During lunch Aunt Augusta enlarged upon the subject. "Without a word, and solely in order to allay my anxiety, he gave up what I know to be one of the proudest moments one's school-days have to offer."

"Was it a good report, William?" said Mrs Brown with tactless incredulity.

William turned to her an expressionless face. "We aren't allowed to look at 'em," he said virtuously. "He tells us to bring 'em home without lookin' at 'em."

"But I could tell it was a good report," said Aunt Augusta.

Suddenly her face beamed. "I know! Could you write to the headmaster and ask for a duplicate?"

William's face was a classic mask of horror. "No, don't do that, don't do that. I – I – I – I shun't like to give 'em so much trouble in the holidays."

Aunt Augusta put her hand caressingly on his stubbly head. "Dear boy," she said.

William escaped after lunch, but before he joined the Outlaws, he went to the wood and ground firmly into the mud with his heel whatever traces of the torn report could be seen.

It was tea-time when he returned. Aunt Augusta had departed. His father was reading a book. William hovered about uneasily for some minutes.

Then Mr Brown, without raising his eyes,

said, "Funny thing, you getting lost in Croombe Wood, William. I should have thought you knew every inch of it. Never been lost in it before, have you?"

"No," said William, and then, after a short silence, "I say . . . Father."

"Yes," said Mr Brown.

"Are you – are you really goin' to write for another report?"

"What sort of a report actually was the one you lost?" said Mr Brown, fixing him with a gimlet eye. "Was it a very bad one?"

William bore the gimlet eye rather well. "We aren't allowed to look at 'em, you know," he said again, innocently. "I told you, we're told to bring 'em straight home."

Mr Brown was silent for a minute. He wasn't a mercenary man, but he couldn't help being glad of the miraculously good impression that William had made on his only rich unmarried aunt. "I don't believe," he said slowly, "that there's the slightest atom of doubt, but I'll give you the benefit of it all the same."

William leapt exultantly down the garden and across the fields to meet the Outlaws.

They heard him singing a quarter of a mile away.

The Outlaws
and the Penknife

Ginger's Aunt Amelia had only lately come to live in the neighbourhood. She had taken a cottage, which she shared with a literary friend, and high financial hopes had sprung to life in Ginger's breast at their arrival. For Aunt Amelia had not seen him since his babyhood, and she was not conversant with his many crimes and shortcomings.

Her first visit to tea passed off very well, and Ginger was rewarded for the strain that he had undergone by a half-crown that Aunt Amelia pressed into his hand as he said good-bye, and by overhearing her say as he closed the door, "What a well-behaved boy!"

So far so good. The half-crown was received by the Outlaws (who always shared tips) with acclamation. But it was soon spent, and Ginger, and the Outlaws, realised he must get to work again and go very carefully.

The next afternoon, Ginger found Aunt Amelia working in her garden while, seated at an open window overlooking the tiny lawn, the literary friend sat engaged in literary work.

Ginger had never met the literary friend, only seen her in the distance like this, intent upon her work. The literary friend wrote stories about an imaginary little boy called Michael – stories that were very much admired by elderly maiden ladies – but she disliked children in real life.

"No, dear," she had said to Ginger's aunt, "don't introduce him to me. I find that real children absolutely *kill* my inspiration. There's no spiritual *fragrance* about them. I find that *nothing* kills my inspiration as much as a real child. I draw my inspiration from Nature alone."

Aunt Amelia greeted Ginger kindly, but abstractedly. It was evident that her whole attention was concentrated upon her gardening operations. With a small knife she was severing shoots from the base of the rose bushes.

"They're briar shoots, dear boy," she explained. "If allowed to grow, they would

take all the goodness from the rose bush and finally kill it. It's a parable, isn't it, dear boy? These little briar shoots are like the little faults that, if we allowed them to grow, would finally take all the goodness from our characters . . ."

"Did you come for anything special, dear boy?" she added.

"Yes," said Ginger, thinking of the half-crown. Then he added hastily, "No, I mean no. I mean – I mean I jus' came to see you."

"Very sweet of you, dear boy," said Aunt Amelia vaguely, "But I have to go in and write some letters now, so I'll say goodbye."

"Well?" said the Outlaws. "How much did she give you?"

"Nothin'," said Ginger morosely.

"Oh, well," said William. "Let's go an' do somethin' a bit more interestin'. We don't want her rotten old half-crown, anyway."

But a sense of failure nagged at Ginger's heart – an overmastering desire to return to the fray and prove himself victor. When he could hold out against this desire no longer, he set off to Aunt Amelia's cottage. He found it deserted.

Ginger looked about him. Surely Aunt Amelia, confronted on her return by some definite service performed for her in her absence by Ginger, would hardly have the nerve to withhold an honorarium.

He remembered suddenly the task upon which Aunt Amelia had been engaged on his last visit. He remembered one fact – that she had been cutting off shoots from the base of the rose bushes.

It was fortunate that it was his week for the Knife. The Knife was a magnificent affair with four blades, a corkscrew, a file, and a thing for getting stones out of a horse's hoof. William and Ginger shared it. It was their most treasured possession, and they had it for a week each in turn. This week it happened to be Ginger's week.

Proudly, he took out the treasure, opened

the largest blade, and set to work upon the rose shoots.

It was while he was at work upon the last bush that Aunt Amelia returned. She stood for a moment transfixed with horror, gazing at the scene of desolation, then, with a cry of rage and anguish, flung herself upon the astonished Ginger, snatching the knife from his hand.

"You *wretch*!" she screamed. "You've *ruined* my rose trees – *ruined* them! You hateful, *hateful* little wretch!"

She shook Ginger till his teeth chattered, then pushed him from her with a gesture of abhorrence and bent over the heap of rose shoots in an attitude of abandoned despair.

Ginger, who thought that she had suddenly gone mad and was feeling thankful to be escaping with his life, had picked himself up and reached the gate when suddenly he remembered the Knife.

"Please," said Ginger hoarsely, "can I have my knife back?"

Aunt Amelia swung round on him. "No, you mayn't," she said hysterically. "*Never*. You shall *never* have your knife back. You wicked wicked boy!"

"We've gotter get it back," William said firmly to the Outlaws ten minutes later. "We can't go on lettin' her keep a knife like that. I shun't be surprised if it was all jus' a trick to *get* that knife."

"It's no good me goin' to her," said Ginger

hastily, "she'll only go ravin' mad again if she sees me, an' start shakin' my head off again. It's not myself I'm thinkin' of, it's her. I don't want her to get hung for murder same as she would if she killed me. I'm not frightened of her. It's only I don't want her to get hung for murder."

So the next morning, William set off (alone) to Aunt Amelia's cottage. He walked up the path and knocked at the cottage door.

A woman with short grey hair, wearing horn-rimmed spectacles and a soulful expression, opened it. Now William had not seen Ginger's aunt, and it never occurred to him that this was not she.

He could not know, of course, that Ginger's aunt had gone out to do some shopping, and that this was the literary friend. Nor could he know that the literary friend was expecting a child interviewer – the son of an enterprising woman editor who was featuring a series of interviews of famous writers of children's books by children, or, to be precise, by her own child.

The child was a highbrow boy of eleven whose efforts, especially after the maternal touchings up, read extremely well.

"Come in, dear boy," said the literary friend, throwing the door wide and holding out both hands to clasp his. "This is a treat, indeed! How splendid of you to get here so early! Come into my little sanctum."

The bewildered William followed her into the sanctum. Ginger must have misjudged her. He sat down guardedly upon the edge of a chair and stared at her blankly.

"Now, dear," said the literary friend brightly, "I want you to call me Flavia. That's the name all my writing friends call me by, and *you're* one of my writing friends, you know. I think you write so well, dear boy. I did so much enjoy that last thing of yours."

William was touched and gratified. He was aware that Ginger possessed a copy of his story *Dick of the Bloody Hand*, but he did not know that he had shown it to his aunt.

He smiled self-consciously. "Oh, well, I'm glad you liked it."

"Of *course* I liked it, dear boy," gushed Flavia.

She was hoping for great things from the interview, and she knew that a lot depended on what impression she made on the boy who was to write it.

"Now, dear boy . . ."

"Yes," said William eagerly. He felt much

encouraged by the tone of the interview, but he was aware that even so he must go carefully. He decided to lead up to the subject of the knife slowly and gradually.

"You like my little boykins?" went on Flavia coyly.

William thought this an odd way of referring to Ginger, but there was no doubt at all that Ginger's aunt was a very odd person.

"Oh yes," he said, "I'm his greatest friend."

"How sweet of you to say that!" purred Flavia.

"Though achsherlly he doesn't know much about gard'nin', but he means to help, and p'raps he makes some mistakes—"

"But he does know about gardening," said Flavia rather indignantly. "He's got one of those sweet child souls that are born with a sort of understanding of Nature."

William blinked helplessly. "He doesn't understand roses very well. He doesn't know when to chop 'em off, but he wants to learn. He—"

"Roses!" ejaculated Flavia. "But, my dear boy, surely you remember the rose garden he made and tended with his own hands for the bedridden old lady. She liked a particular copper-coloured rose, you remember, and he took a lot of trouble growing it for her."

William struggled against an overmastering feeling of unreality. "Not Ginger," he said weakly.

"I didn't say ginger," snapped Flavia, losing her poise for a moment. "There isn't such a thing as a ginger rose. I said copper-coloured."

William tried to reconcile this anecdote with what he knew of the history and character of Ginger. "I don't remember jus' that," he said at last. "I remember once we found a dead cat an' we tucked it up in old General Moult's rose bed to make him come runnin' down to scare it off, an' he did an'—"

Flavia had risen with an abrupt movement. She had herself well under control, however. She remembered that in the hands of this coarse and objectionable boy lay her reputation, as far as the interview was concerned.

She took a piece of paper from a drawer and thrust it into his hands.

"I think that if you will incorporate this in the article, dear boy," she said, fixing a glassy smile on him, "I needn't detain you any longer. It's a short summary of my aims and ideals. And I have a little present for you."

She stopped and considered. It would never do to give this boy the present that she had purchased – a charming little picture called *Flower Fairies*.

For a second, she stood frowning uncertainly. However uncouth he seemed, he had written some quite good articles on the writers of children's books and his praise was worth something.

Suddenly her face cleared and she went from the room, returning in a few moments with something in her hand that made William's eyes gleam.

"Take this, dear boy," she said. "It

belonged to a tiresome, destructive child who maimed some of the beautiful things of Nature with it. I'm sure you'll make better use of it."

Speechless with amazement, bewilderment and joy, William snatched the Knife and, murmuring incoherent thanks, departed with it abruptly, running as fast as he could to the old barn.

*

"Got it," said William breathlessly, brandishing his booty.

"How did you get it? Did you plead with her?" said Ginger.

William thought back over the curious interview which had culminated in the recovery of the Knife. "She *is* mad," he said at last, solemnly. "She said you'd made a rose out of copper for an old woman."

"*Me?*" said Ginger.

"Yes. She was ravin' like that all the time. An' she gave me these papers . . . what she wrote."

"Anyway, we've got the Knife back," said Ginger. He had taken up the carefully written script and was studying it. "Fancy her writin' all this stuff, wastin' good paper!"

"We won't waste it," said William. "Let's make it into paper boats an' have a race on the stream with 'em."

Ginger's aunt had returned from her shopping expedition. "I suppose he's not been yet, dear, has he?" she said, eagerly.

The literary friend was sitting at her desk, her head on her hands. She raised a haggard face. "Yes, dear, he's been," she said brokenly. "And never have I seen a child so utterly, *utterly* devoid of spiritual fragrance. The delicacy, the *atmosphere* of my work meant nothing to him."

But Aunt Amelia's eyes were fixed upon the garden gate. "Who's that?" she said.

A boy was coming in at the garden gate. He carried an attaché case and wore gloves and spectacles. He looked pale and aesthetic and intellectual. He exuded spiritual fragrance from every pore.

Behind him, beaming maternal pride, came a woman whom Flavia recognised as the editor of the journal.

Aunt Amelia and the literary friend stared at them in helpless bewilderment . . .

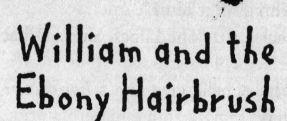

William and the Ebony Hairbrush

"Robert's had an eb'ny hairbrush for a birthday present," said William.

"What's eb'ny?" said Ginger.

"It's a sort of black wood," said William.

"There isn't such a thing as black wood," objected Ginger. "Wood's brown, same as dining-room tables. There isn't any other sort."

"Yes, there is," said William. "There's eb'ny."

"Go on, then. Show it us," said Henry.

"How can I?" said William testily. "It's in Robert's bedroom, an' he'd make an awful fuss if I took you in."

"Who gave it him?"

"That girl at The Lilacs. Sheila What's-her-name."

"Why did she give him a *hairbrush*?" said Douglas.

"He wanted it," said William. He spoke sadly, as one deploring the degeneracy of a fellow creature. "He saw her father's once, an' he said what a fine one it was, an' so now she's sent him one jus' like it, for a birthday present."

"Well, bring it," Henry said, "an' then we can see what it is."

"How can I? When he's not brushin' his hair with it, he's standin' lookin' at it with a soppy sort of smile. Seems to think no one's ever had an eb'ny hairbrush before."

"An' I bet they've not," said Ginger darkly.

"All right," said William, "I'll jolly well bring it."

The next day it turned out that Robert was

going to spend the afternoon with a friend, so William seized the opportunity, took the ebony hairbrush from his bedroom and hurried down to the old barn.

He found the Outlaws already convinced, for Henry had made enquiries.

"Eb'ny *is* a wood," said Henry.

"Well, I said it was, di'n't I?" said William. "Anyway, here it is."

They examined it with interest. "Yes, it's

eb'ny," they agreed. "'S black wood, all right."

William felt his honour to be vindicated.

After a satisfactory afternoon, William set off for home. He always found a journey along a straight road rather dull. The diversion he introduced on this occasion was that of balancing the hairbrush on his head.

The road led along the river and reached the point where stepping-stones crossed the river at a shallow spot.

He stepped on to the first stone without mishap.

He passed on to the second step, the ebony hairbrush still secure on his head.

He stepped across to the third stone. And the hairbrush fell into the water.

It was easy enough to recover the hairbrush and to dry the handle. But the bristles were soaked.

The church clock struck five. Robert might be home any minute now. That he should find the precious hairbrush in this state was unthinkable.

Suddenly William remembered that, in her letter, Sheila had said that the hairbrush was "just like Daddy's". If only Daddy's could be substituted for Robert's till Robert's was dry . . . But Mr Barron was away with the rest of the family.

And then William remembered Robert saying that when he admired her father's ebony hairbrush, Sheila had said, "Oh, he's got a much grander one in his dressing-case, but Mummy makes him keep that for going away."

Well, the ebony one just like Robert's might still be on his dressing-table. If he could put it in Robert's bedroom in the place of Robert's till Robert's was dry, all would be well. Mr Barron's would be duly replaced the next day, and the vengeance of an enraged Robert would be averted.

William set off at once to the Barrons' house. And there met with a slight setback, for the Barrons' gardener advanced upon him threateningly. "What you doing here? You git out or I'll half murder you."

William hastily withdrew, but hung about outside. To his relief, the gardener left almost at once from the side gate.

William entered the garden again, climbed up on the verandah roof and slipped back the catch of the window. He pushed up the window.

The room was evidently Mr Barron's dressing-room and there, on the low chest of drawers, which he could just reach, was the ebony hairbrush – exactly like the one he had dropped into the river.

He put the hairbrush into his pocket, closed the window, swarmed down the verandah pillar and ran all the way home.

Robert had not yet returned. William crept up to his brother's bedroom and put the hairbrush on Robert's dressing-table. It looked a little dusty so he took out his handkerchief and wiped it all over.

The next day William waited till Robert had gone out, then replaced his brother's own hairbrush, now quite dry and presentable. The next step was to return Mr Barron's hairbrush.

William took it up gingerly by the bristles, wrapped it in his handkerchief, made his way to the Lilacs and replaced it without accident on Mr Barron's dressing-table, holding it again by the bristles.

And that as far as William was concerned, was the end of the incident. He had completely forgotten it by the end of the month when the Barrons came back.

Robert went round on the evening of their return, and found the whole family in a state of great excitement.

All the silver had been stolen during their absence, and a police detective was already on the spot. The thief had broken a pane of glass in the door that led out on to the verandah, and then put his hand in to turn the key.

"Only one clue, as far as we can make out," the detective was saying. "The thief – whoever he was – left fingerprints on the hairbrush in

Mr Barron's dressing-room. They're not Mr Barron's, anyway, or anyone else's in the house. He evidently stood at the dressing-table and brushed his hair."

Robert had drawn Sheila apart to thank her for his hairbrush. But she was more interested in the robbery. "Isn't it strange," she said, "that the only fingerprints were left on Daddy's hairbrush? I wonder if we shall ever catch the thief. The detective looks awfully clever, don't you think?"

A pang of jealousy shot through Robert's heart, and suddenly a brilliant idea occurred to him.

He'd read enough detective stories to know that it is the amateur detective, *never* the professional one, who brings the criminal to justice. Also, the amateur detective is invariably rewarded by the hand of the beautiful heroine.

Robert decided to seize this role before anyone else appropriated it. He approached the detective, who was still holding the list of stolen silver. "Excuse me, may I look at the list?"

The detective handed him the sheet of paper.

Robert read over the list in silence and handed it back to the detective. He must now start at once upon his task of bringing the criminal to justice.

He assumed an air that was easy and natural, yet at the same time purposeful – the air, in fact, of the amateur detective of fiction.

He was momentarily disconcerted to find that he had left a smudge on the paper that the detective had handed him.

"So sorry," he said, as he handed it back. "It's my wretched motorcycle . . . Well, I'll be getting along."

He departed, leaving the detective staring at the sheet of paper that had just been put into his hand . . .

William was sitting astride the roof of the tool-shed, when Sheila arrived, breathless.

"Where's Robert?"

"Dunno," said William.

"Robert's in danger, terrible danger."

That sounded rather exciting, so William scrambled down. "How's he in danger?"

"There's been a burglary at home, and they've proved that Robert did it."

"Gosh!" said William, "Not *Robert*. He couldn't have."

"But he *did*. They've got proof."

"What proof've they got?"

"Oh, I haven't time to go into all that! Every minute's precious. He doesn't know that he's even suspected. We must warn him. We must hide him. We must get him out of the country . . ."

Sheila was enjoying the situation. Robert had risen immensely in her esteem. He wasn't, after all, the shy and awkward youth he had appeared to be. He was a daring criminal – a king, perhaps, of the underworld . . . The Scarlet Pimpernel . . . And she would be one of those cool, dauntless heroines who risk their lives several times a day to save their lovers from justice . . .

"*Gosh*!" William was saying. "Fancy ole Robert!"

"If only we knew where he *was*," groaned Sheila.

"I wonder how they found out," said William. "I bet that gardener told 'em."

"What gardener?"

"Your gardener. I – I – er – passed the house when you were away, an' he was there an' I bet he saw Robert do it an' told them."

"But he couldn't have been there while we were away," said Sheila. "Daddy had given him the sack before we went away, and told him never to go near the place again. He'd been stealing vegetables and selling them."

It was at this moment that Robert returned. He had been for a ride on his motorcycle to think out a solution, but no solution to the mystery had occurred to him.

"Oh, Robert!" cried Sheila hysterically. "They know . . . they know everything."

"Do they?" said Robert, slightly disappointed. "How did they find out?"

Sheila couldn't help admiring him. So calm and debonair. "Never mind that now," she said. "But they know. You must fly, Robert. Fly at once."

"Me?" said the astounded Robert. "Fly? Where? What? Why?"

"Anywhere. We'll help you. We'll try to put them off the scent. Now that they know you stole the silver, they—"

"*Me?*" interrupted Robert. "*Me?* Stole the *silver?*"

They looked at him in silence. Even they could see that he wasn't acting. He hadn't stolen the silver . . .

"Di'n't you do it then?" said William.

"'Course I didn't. Don't be such a darn little fool."

"Well then we must *prove* you didn't," said Sheila. It was, after all, *almost* as exciting. The wrongly suspected lover. The brave girl, giving herself no rest till she had proved his innocence.

William, too, was reconciling himself to the slightly less alluring position. "Well, then, we've gotter find who did it," he said.

"B-but why should they think I did it?" gasped Robert. "I've never been near the place."

"They've found your fingerprints," said Sheila. "The thing to do now is to get you out of the country."

"What? B-b-but, I say, you *do* believe I didn't, don't you?"

"Of course I do."

"Well, look here," said William, "if Robert didn't, someone else did. And – I say – the gardener man might have seen someone hanging about."

"Why, yes," said Sheila, "that's what we'll do. We'll hide Robert here and we'll go to the gardener's cottage and ask him if he saw anyone."

"Where shall we hide Robert?" She glanced

round and noticed the coal-shed. "Let's hide him there, and lock him in."

The unhappy Robert, still protesting, was pushed into the coal-shed and the key turned on him.

Sheila and William arrived at the gardener's cottage, went up to the little green door and knocked. There was no answer. They knocked again.

"Wait," said William. "If I climb the tree, I bet I can see in."

He climbed the tree quickly. And through the chink at the top of the curtains he could see the gardener quite plainly.

He had taken up several boards in the floor of his kitchen and made some sort of excavation beneath, and into this cavity he was carefully transferring some shiny things from a sack . . .

The tumult and shouting had died. The silver had been recovered. The gardener was safely under lock and key.

Robert, rescued from the coal-shed, was hoarsely, from beneath a thick film of coal-dust, demanding explanations from everybody around him.

William, who had discovered the real culprit, and fetched the police to the spot, was preening himself as the hero of the occasion. Scotland Yard ought to give him a medal or something . . .

"But why should you have suspected *me*?" Robert was demanding wildly.

"Well, sir," said the detective, "we found your fingerprints – they were quite plain – on Mr Barron's hairbrush."

"On Mr Barron's hairbrush!"

Then William *remembered* the incident of the ebony hairbrush, remembered how carefully he had carried it back by its bristles, understood how the whole horrible misunderstanding had happened . . .

"I've no doubt that there's some simple explanation of it, Robert," said Mr Barron rather mildly, "but the fact remains that your fingerprints were found on my hairbrush."

Robert looked round the group and noticed the figure of William quietly sloping off. And, suddenly, he remembered a week or so ago, thinking that his ebony hairbrush wasn't just where it had been when he'd left it . . .

The ebony hairbrush.

He sprang forward, clutched William by the collar and dragged him back. "Now," he said grimly, "you tell us all you know about this."

William surrendered to the inevitable. He looked at the circle of tense interested faces around him. He was the centre of the stage, and William always enjoyed being the centre of the stage.

And, anyway, he could postpone Robert's vengeance by spinning the tale out indefinitely. He was an expert at doing that.

He assumed a bland innocent expression.

"Well," he began, "It wasn't really my fault, but the way it happened was this . . ."

William and the Real Laurence

William was walking jauntily along the road from Hadley. The usual summer fair was visiting the town, and William had spent a very enjoyable afternoon riding upon merry-go-rounds, flying in flying boats, and sliding down helter-skelters. He was dishevelled and penniless but blissfully happy.

He was just indulging in a pleasant daydream, in which an enlightened parliament had decreed that every boy must attend a fair instead of school, when he almost ran into another boy who stood gazing wistfully in the direction of the fairground.

"I say," the boy said, "is that a fair down there?"

"Yip," answered William through a mouthful of elastic toffee.

"You just been to it?"

"Yip."

"How long is it going on?"

"Today's the last day."

The boy looked at William and the light of a great purpose began to shine in his eye. "Would you like a jolly good tea?" he said. "Lots of iced cakes and chocolate biscuits and jelly an' nice things like that?"

"You bet," said William.

"Would you like me to tell you how to get it?"

"You bet," said William again.

"Well, it's like this. I've come over here by train from Allington to have tea with my godmother, who's staying in Hadley. Well, I jolly well want to go to this fair. You've been to the fair, so if you'll go and have tea at my godmother's instead of me, I can go to the fair and

have a jolly nice time."

"But she'll know I'm not you," objected William.

"No, she won't. She's never seen me since I was a baby. She's been living in Australia for years. Go on. She'll give you a jolly fine tea. Jelly and trifle and chocolate biscuits and iced cakes."

William considered the situation in silence. It sounded simple enough, but he had learnt from experience to distrust situations that sounded simple.

The boy gazed longingly down the road in the direction of the fair. "Be a sport," he pleaded. "I'll get into an awful row if I don't go. She'll never know it's not me. She's only come over to England for a visit so prob'ly she'll never see me again. Go on. She might give you a tip."

William was weakening, influenced less by the thought of the tea and the tip than by the strong spice of adventure that the situation contained. "All right," he said. "Tell me where she lives an' I'll do it."

The boy gave a whoop of joy, took a letter from his pocket, thrust it at William and set off at a run down the road towards the fair.

"Hi!" shouted William. "I don't know your name."

Faintly the breeze brought back a name that sounded like "Laurence Redwood", but already the boy was out of sight.

William gazed at the letter. It was addressed to Mrs Maddox, Mount Cottage, East Road,

Hadley. He pulled up his socks and made his way apprehensively to East Road.

The door was opened by a motherly looking woman who was evidently Mrs Maddox herself. "It's Laurence, isn't it?" she greeted him, with a beaming smile. "Come in, dear. Nice to see you after all these years."

William entered, experiencing a swift sinking of the heart as the door closed behind him. Mrs Maddox, however, was still smiling at

him benignly with her head on one side.

"I saw you last when you were about two months old, love. And I do believe I can still see the likeness. I believe I'd have almost recognised you again, wouldn't you Charles?"

Evidently there was a Mr Maddox. A sun-tanned, white-haired man had joined her in the hall and was also surveying William with smiling interest.

"How d'you do, Laurence?" said Mr Maddox genially. "Very nice to see you. Have you come by train?"

"No," said William and hastily corrected it to, "Yes."

"And he's brought a nice long letter from his mother," went on Mrs Maddox, "so let's go and sit down in the drawing-room and read it. I'm sure Laurence is tired after his journey."

William fixed a stony stare on them while they read the letter, stealing himself to parry, as best he could, any questions they might ask him.

But Mr Maddox said, "Well, I'm sure Laurence doesn't want to sit here all afternoon telling us about his family. Come in and have some tea, my boy."

William followed them across the hall to the dining-room. And there was spread a feast to which even Laurence's description had failed to do justice. There was fruit salad and blancmange as well as jelly and doughnuts, as well as iced cake and chocolate biscuits.

"You see, I haven't forgotten what boys like," smiled Mrs Maddox. "Now the more you eat the better we'll be pleased, so you can start at once."

William started at once. His host and hostess watched him with obvious pleasure.

"Well, I am glad to see you've got your appetite back, Laurence," said Mrs Maddox. "In your mother's letter she says that you've had a very poor appetite since your attack of influenza, so I was afraid that all my trouble over this tea would be wasted."

"Oh, no," explained William as well as he

could through a mouthful of doughnut. "Oh no, my appetite's come back all right. I sort of felt it come back in the train on my way here."

"That's good," chuckled Mr Maddox.

The whole thing was going off better than William had dared to hope. He even began to have dreams of a fairly substantial tip.

After tea they returned to the drawing-room, and Mr Maddox proceeded to show William his collection of Australian photo-

graphs. Furtively, William watched the clock. Only ten minutes and he could go.

But then he glanced out of the window and saw a sight that froze his blood. Miss Milton, a friend of his mother's, was coming up the path to the front door. William's eyes bulged with horror. "I – I – I've gotter go now. I've gotter train to catch. Now, at once."

But he was too late.

Miss Milton shook hands with her hostess, explaining that she had a cousin who knew a friend of Mrs Maddox, who had asked her to call.

Then she threw a cold glance at William – for relations between them were not cordial – and said, "Well, William, I didn't expect to find you here."

William himself was past speech but Mrs Maddox said, "This is Laurence Redwood, my godson. He's just come over from Allington to have tea with us."

Miss Milton looked at William in indignant amazement. William met her gaze with an utterly expressionless countenance.

"But," began Miss Milton, "I could have sworn—. What did you say his name was?"

"Laurence Redwood."

"And he's your godson?"

"Yes."

Her doubt deepened. She could have sworn that it was William Brown, but, after all, this woman must know her own godson.

She looked at William again. It was astounding, but . . . The last flicker of doubt died away. She must write a letter to the *Daily Torch*. She must get photographs of the two boys and send them.

"Do you know," she burst out, "I know a boy who's the exact image of your godson. His name's William Brown." She turned to William. "Perhaps he's some relation of yours?"

William, who had now rallied his forces, shook his head. "No," he said. "I've never heard of him."

"But it's simply *remarkable*. I – I really must

bring this boy to you, so that you can see the likeness. I'll go straight back for him now. He lives quite close to my home. You really *must* see these two boys together. It's literally a phenomenon."

She shook hands with the bewildered Mr and Mrs Maddox, and took her departure.

"I've gotter go now," said William as soon as she had vanished.

But at that moment the telephone rang, and Mrs Maddox went to answer it.

"That was your mother, dear," she said, when she returned. "I'm afraid that Sybil's got scarlet fever."

"Sybil?" repeated William blankly.

"Yes. She's the sister next to you, isn't she?"

"Yes. Oh, yes."

"So I'm afraid you'll have to be in quarantine. They sent for the doctor, and he says that you must be in quarantine. So I said you might as well stay and spend your quarantine with us, because your mother will have her hands full with Sybil and the baby and the others.

67

You'll be one less to look after at home, anyway, won't you?"

William's eyes were glassy with horror. "Yes," he said weakly, "yes."

"So I said you can stay quietly with us till your quarantine is over. She's going to send your things round tomorrow.

"And you know, dear boy, I think the best thing for you to do now is to have a hot carbolic bath and go straight to bed. You can have one of my husband's night-shirts till your things come."

William stared about him wildly. He was picturing the real Laurence innocently returning to a home which fondly imagined him settled down to a peaceful quarantine with the Maddoxes.

He was picturing his own parents searching for him with anxious fury when he failed to return from the fair in time for supper. There must be some way out of the situation.

He still hadn't thought of it when Mrs Maddox came back to tell him the carbolic bath was ready. He still hadn't thought of it when he sat in bed in a strange room arrayed in one of Mr Maddox's night-gowns, and Mrs Maddox stood by him folding up his clothes.

"I'll take them down when I bring up your supper, dear, and give them a good baking."

Being left alone in the strange bedroom, with no protection against the world but Mr Maddox's night-gown, spurred William on to desperate action.

He sprang out of bed, hastily put on his clothes, and, opening the window, swarmed down the drainpipe with a skill born of long practice.

The idea of escaping to his own home was a tempting one, but he felt a certain responsibility towards the absent Laurence. He must find him.

He set off to the fairground, running so fast that he did not see a woman coming towards him. She caught him by the arm. It was Miss Milton.

"I've just been to your home for you,

William," she exclaimed, "but they said you hadn't come back from the fair yet. I want you to come with me, dear boy, because I've discovered another boy who bears an almost miraculous likeness to you."

She drew him forcefully back to the house from which he had just escaped.

The door was opened by Mr Maddox. He stared at William in amazement. "Here's Laurence, dear," he called over his shoulder.

"It can't be Laurence," his wife's voice replied from the drawing-room. "Laurence is in bed. I've just left him there."

"No," said Miss Milton triumphantly. "It's not Laurence. It's William Brown, that boy I told you about. Now, isn't the likeness astonishing?" She turned to Mrs Maddox, who had now come into the hall. "Literally astonishing?"

"B – but it *is* Laurence," gasped Mrs Maddox.

"No, that's just the astonishing part. It isn't Laurence. You've told us yourself that

Laurence is in bed upstairs. Besides, I know this boy well. His mother's a friend of mine. Tell them what your name is, dear."

"William Brown," said William, gazing in front of him with a glassy stare.

Miss Maddox looked at him. "It's – it's extraordinary," she said faintly. "You – you'd swear it was Laurence. Come upstairs and look at Laurence. Very quietly, because he may be asleep by now. And don't go right into the room, because he's in quarantine for scarlet fever."

William looked desperately round for escape, but already he was ascending the stairs with Mrs Maddox in front of him and Miss Milton behind. Softly, Mrs Maddox opened the bedroom door and peeped in.

"He's – not there," she said. She turned to William. "Y – you must be Laurence," she cried distractedly.

"But I tell you I've known this boy all his life," persisted Miss Milton. "His name's William Brown."

Suspicion was changing to certainty in Mrs Maddox's eyes.

"Well, all I can say is he's the boy who—"

William saw that there was nothing for it but flight. He plunged down the stairs. The front door was open, but a boy stood there blocking his way.

The boy grabbed him. "I say, where are you off to?" he said.

He no longer looked neat and debonair. He

looked dusty and dishevelled as befitted a boy who had spent the afternoon gloriously at a fair. But it was indubitably the real Laurence.

Mrs Maddox and Miss Milton had now arrived on the scene.

The boy was making profuse apologies to William. "I'm terribly sorry to come barging in and messing everything up like this," he said, "but I've spent all my money at the fair and lost my return ticket, so I simply had to come."

Mrs Maddox raised her hand to her head. "Who is *this* boy?" she said in a faint voice.

"I'm Laurence Redwood," said the new-comer.

"Then who," said Mrs Maddox, pointing to William, "is *this* boy?"

"I don't know," said the real Laurence. "He's just a boy I met in the road. You see, I wanted to go to the fair, and he wanted a good tea and so, you see, we swapped. And it would have been all right if I hadn't spent all my money and lost my return ticket."

Mr Maddox had come out of the drawing-room and, in the tense silence that followed Laurence's explanation, he suddenly began to chuckle. His wife joined in, and their mirth grew almost uncontrollable.

"Oh, dear," said Mrs Maddox, wiping her eyes, "nothing does you as much good as a good laugh, does it? Well that's the best tale I've heard for a long time. No, it wouldn't have been all right, Laurence, because Sybil's got scarlet fever, and you've got to stop here a bit till your quarantine's over."

"Oh, well, that's all right," said Laurence, who was evidently something of a philosopher.

He turned to William. "How did you get on?"

Mr Maddox began to chuckle again. "He got on beautifully," he said.

"So your name really *is* William Brown?" said Mrs Maddox to William.

"Yes."

"Well, well, well! You took us in nicely. I

shall never forget it as long as I live. Now
come in all of you and have supper. There's a
cold chicken, and William didn't finish all the
trifle and jelly at tea-time, though he did his
best. I'll ring your mother and tell her,
William. Will you stay to supper, Miss
Milton?"

"No, thank you," said Miss Milton coldly.
She was feeling distinctly annoyed by the dis-
covery of the identity of William and
Laurence. She had been looking forward to

her first appearance in print and had got a really striking letter on the subject of "doubles" already put together in her mind.

They stood at the door watching her prim, irate figure till it had disappeared from view. Then Mr and Mrs Maddox began to chuckle again.

And Laurence, and William, joined in . . .

Meet Just William
Adapted by Martin Jarvis
Illustrated by Tony Ross

Just William as you've never seen him before.

A wonderful new series of Just William books, each containing
four of his funniest stories – all specially adapted for younger
readers by Martin Jarvis, the famous "voice of William" on radio
and best-selling audio cassette.

Meet Just William and the long-suffering Brown family, as well as
the Outlaws, Violet Elizabeth Bott and a host of other favourite
characters in these six hilarious books.

Richmal Crompton
Just William and Other Animals

"You can't have another dog, William," said Mrs Brown firmly,
"you've got one."
　　"Well it's at the vet's an' I want a dog to be going on with."

William has a certain affinity with members of the animal kingdom.
In fact, some would say that William is rather like his furry friends.
And he would do anything to help an animal in distress (unless it's
a cat).

Champion of canine causes, defender of innocent rodents,
avenger of bestial wrongs – no tormentor of rats or pups is safe
when William Brown is around . . .

Ten classic stories of William – and other animals.

"Probably the funniest, toughest children's books ever written"
Sunday Times

Richmal Crompton
Just William at Christmas

Christmas is a time for peace, joy and goodwill. But William's
presence has never been known to enhance the spirit of the
season.

Whether he's wrecking the Sunday School's carol singing outing,
standing in as Santa Claus for the Old Folk, or making a
Christmas plant pot out of Ethel's hat, William somehow manages
to spread chaos wherever he goes.

Ten unforgettable stories of William at Christmas, with the original
illustrations by Thomas Henry.

Richmal Crompton
Just William at School

"School's not nat'ral at all," said William. "Still, I don't suppose
they'd let us give it up altogether, 'cause of schoolmasters havin'
to have something to do."

School is fertile ground for a boy of William's infinite trouble-
making talent. Especially when he'd rather not be there at all.
Whether he's feigning illness to avoid a test, campaigning for the
abolition of Latin and Arithmetic, or breaking into Ole Fathead's
house in pursuit of justice, William brings muddle and mayhem to
anyone who tries to teach him a lesson.

Ten classic stories of William at school – and trying desperately to
get out of it!

Richmal Crompton
Just Jimmy

"I'm not a kid," Jimmy said stoutly. "I'm seven and three-quarters and four d-days and a n-night."

Meet Jimmy Manning – a boy in a hurry to grow up, especially if it means he can join his brother Roger's gang, the Three Musketeers.

Whether he's waging war on arch-enemies the Mouldies, plotting to catch criminals with his best friend Bobby Peaslake, or fighting off the attentions of the dreaded Araminta, Jimmy's plans are always ingenious, hilarious – and destined for disaster!

First published in 1949 and lost for decades, Just Jimmy is a rediscovered classic from the creator of Just William.

Collect all the titles in the
MEET JUST WILLIAM series!

The prices shown below are correct at the time of going to press. However, Macmillan Publishers reserve the right to show new retail prices on covers which may differ from those previously advertised.

All *Meet Just William* titles can be ordered at your local bookshop or are available by post from:

Book Service by Post
PO Box 29, Douglas, Isle of Man IM99 1BQ
Credit cards accepted. For details:
Telephone: 01624 675137
Fax: 01624 670923
E-mail: bookshop@enterprise.net

Free postage and packing in the UK.
Overseas customers: add £1 per book (paperback)
and £3 per book (hardback)